THE ULTIMATE SURVIVAL GUIDE

by Mitch Frost

illustrated by Daron Parton

TO MONSTERS UNDER THE BED

Buster Books

At the Goodnight Laboratory we take the Monsters Under the Bed problem very seriously.

How seriously?

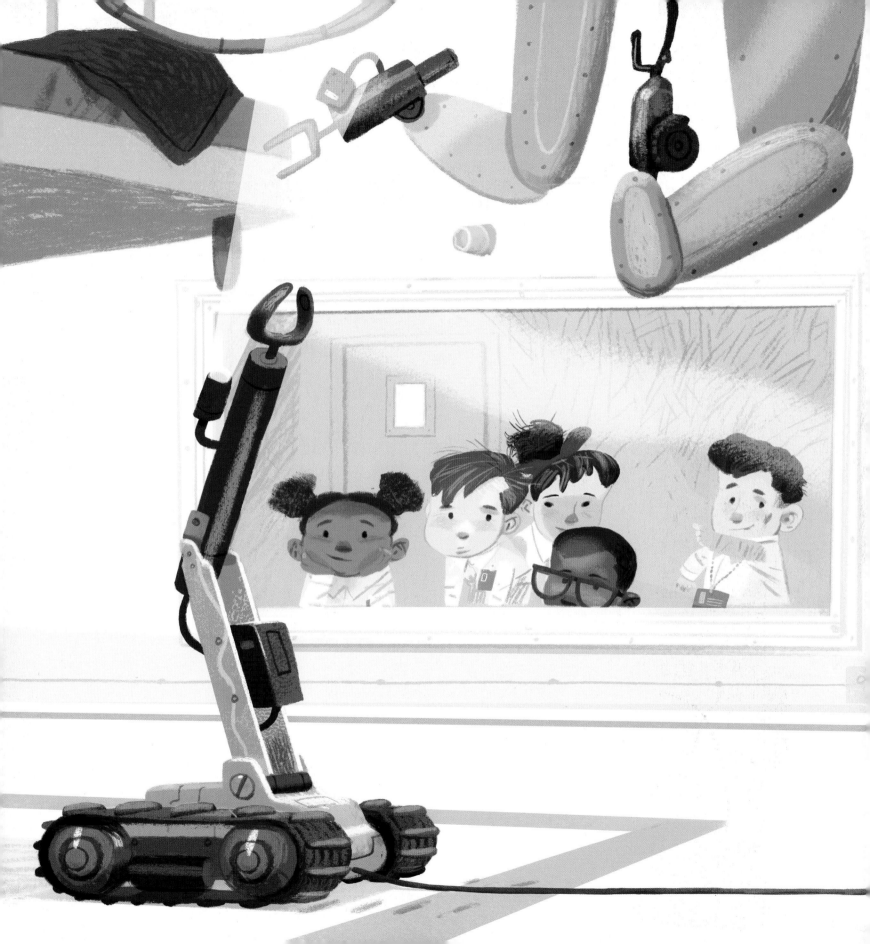

Just look at all those bubbling test tubes, blinking machines and the person holding the 'World's Best Scientist' mug.

That's serious!

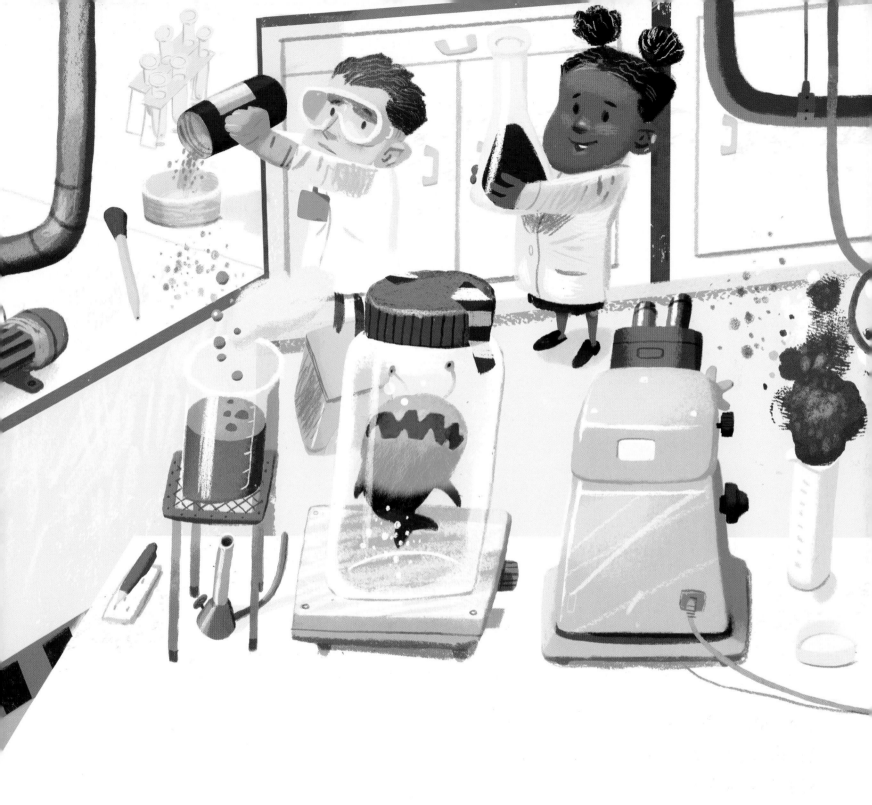

Using only the best (and most serious) science,
we have now developed ...

But does it work?

Our labs have tested these techniques on all types of monsters, including round monsters, square monsters, flat monsters, hungry monsters, blue monsters and even carrot monsters.

Trust us. By following these steps you will get rid of all monsters, all the time.

Guaranteed.

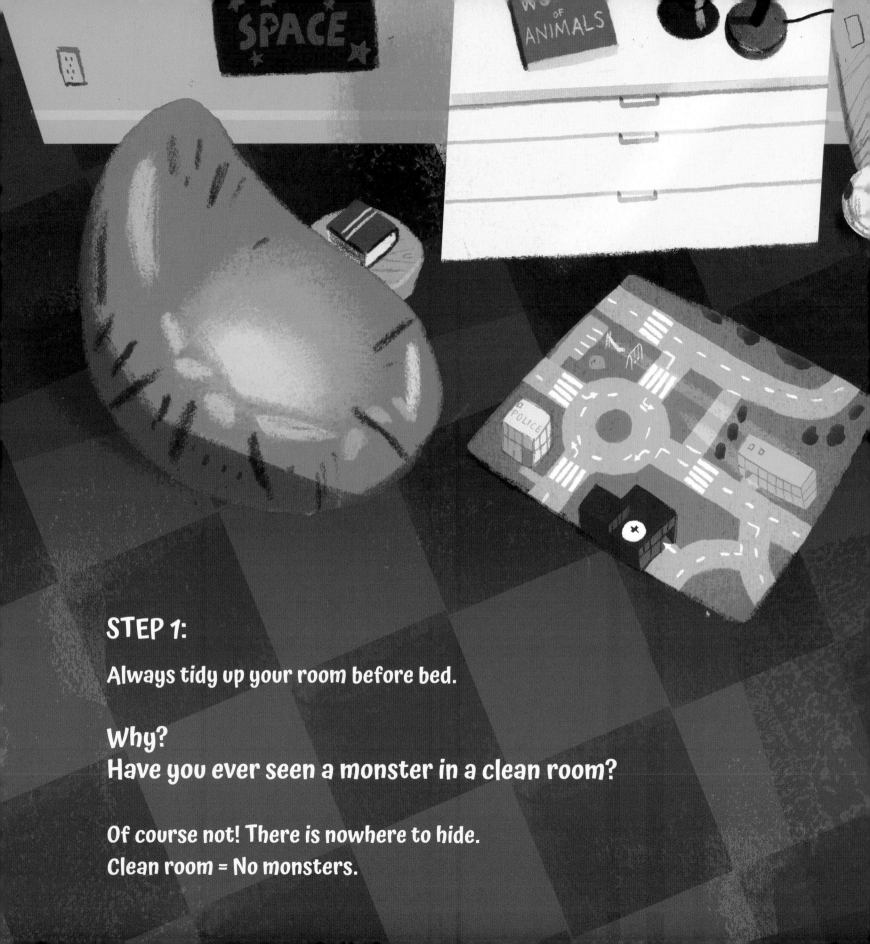

STEP 1:

Always tidy up your room before bed.

Why?
Have you ever seen a monster in a clean room?

Of course not! There is nowhere to hide.
Clean room = No monsters.

STEP 2:

Remember to brush your teeth before bed.
Monsters are disgusted by minty-fresh breath.
It reminds them too much of the dentist.

STEP 3: Forget about dancing robot monsters. **They don't exist!**

STEP 4:

Check to make sure your house has lots of soap.

It does?

You are in luck! Our research shows that 99% of smelly monsters hate houses with soap in them. Nothing ruins a monster's day more than falling into a big, SOAPY, bubble bath.

STEP 5:

Before you go to sleep, invite all your toys for a sleepover. Our research shows monsters hate big crowds.

No monster would dare visit with so many friends around.

STEP 6:

Ignore all those hairy monsters.
They spend all night styling their
hair in front of the mirror.

STEP 7:

If you get scared during the night, whisper a silly joke.
If there's a monster around, it will roll away laughing
to go and tell its monster pals.
What can I say? Monsters love a good joke.

One of their absolute favourites is:

Q. Where do monsters go
to get their hair cut?

A. The Scaredresser!

STEP 8:

If you run out of jokes,
pretend you're a snake.

Monsters are terribly scared
of slithery things.

Just one 'hiss' from you and they will be out the door! (Wriggling snake movements work just as well.)

STEP 9:

Never worry about monsters shaped like doughnuts. They are more worried YOU will eat THEM.

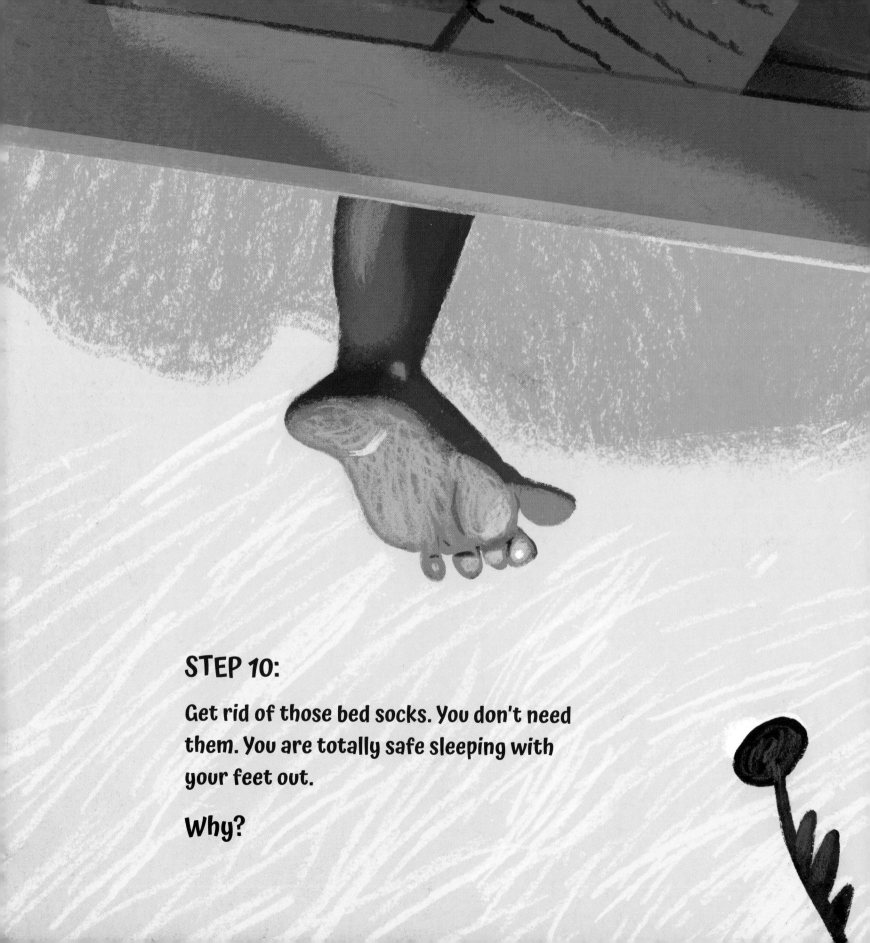

STEP 10:

Get rid of those bed socks. You don't need them. You are totally safe sleeping with your feet out.

Why?

Because you should never, EVER be afraid
of monsters grabbing your ankles.

Their weak arms are only good for wiping their
noses (assuming they have arms or noses).

BONUS:

This book is equipped with our latest invention, the SAFE 5000.
Just close this book to instantly create a super sticky, anti-monster
force field around your entire home. No batteries needed.

If you've followed any of these steps, congratulations!

You can sleep peacefully knowing that your room is now a monster-free zone.

Oh, and here's the best part ...

We are pleased to announce that these steps now work on **cupboard monsters** too!